HOME

DreamWorks

The Story of One Super Boov

adapted by Ellie O'Ryan
illustrated by Pierre Collet-Derby

SIMON SPOTLIGHT
New York   London   Toronto   Sydney   New Delhi

SIMON SPOTLIGHT
An imprint of Simon & Schuster Children's Publishing Division
1230 Avenue of the Americas, New York, New York 10020
First Simon Spotlight paperback edition February 2015
DreamWorks Home © 2015 DreamWorks Animation LLC. All Rights Reserved.
All rights reserved, including the right of reproduction in whole or in part in any form.
SIMON SPOTLIGHT and colophon are registered trademarks of Simon & Schuster, Inc.
For information about special discounts for bulk purchases, please contact
Simon & Schuster Special Sales at 1-866-506-1949
or business @ simonandschuster.com.
Manufactured in the United States of America 1016 LAK
8   9   10
ISBN 978-1-4814-0438-9
ISBN 978-1-4814-0439-6 (eBook)

Captain Smek, leader of the Boov, was taking the Boov to a new planet. The Gorg, their enemy, had just destroyed the last planet the Boov had called home, and the Boov Mothership was almost out of power. Luckily, the Gorg didn't know the new planet existed.

"It is called Earth," said a Big Brain Boov.

"For now . . . ," added Captain Smek.

"Yay!" said a Boov named Oh. "Is this not excitement?"

"Do not fear, humanspersons!" Captain Smek announced to the inhabitants of Earth. "We are simply turning off your gravity to make your mandatory relocation easier and more fun!"

One by one, Foomper Tubes picked up the people of Earth and sent them to the relocation zone, Happy Humanstown.

After renaming the planet Smekland, Captain Smek ordered the Boov to get rid of all the useless junk that humans had left behind. Oh was fascinated by everything, but he also believed that Captain Smek was a genius. If Captain Smek thought it was all useless, then Oh agreed.

The Boov were relocated too . . . to their own apartments! Oh wanted to have a housewarming party, but no one wanted to come. Even Kyle, who Oh *thought* was his friend, refused. Oh decided to e-mail the invitation to Kyle, just in case he changed his mind.

"Fa da!" Oh pressed the send button . . . and all over Smekland, Boovpads started beeping. Oh had sent his e-mail to the *entire* galaxy— including the Gorg—by mistake! If the Gorg read the message, they would know where the Boov lived. Oh was a fugitive.

Oh dashed into a convenience store to hide . . . but he wasn't alone. A human girl named Tip and her pet cat, Pig, were there, too. When the Foomper Tubes picked up the humans, Tip managed to escape, but her mom was relocated. Tip went to the store to get everything she would need to look for her mom—but she wasn't expecting to find a Boov there! She thought Oh was like the other Boov, so she locked him inside a freezer case.

Captain Smek knew that it was urgent to stop Oh's e-mail from reaching the Gorg. A Big Brain Boov suggested logging in to Oh's e-mail account and canceling the invitation. Unlike the other Boov, Oh had chosen a unique password, so they needed Oh to cancel the e-mail himself.

Captain Smek told Kyle, "You know him, you can find him." Then he banged his Shusher, a scepter with a rock on the handle that he used to thump Boov on the head when they made a mistake.

At the convenience store Tip realized that Oh was different from the other Boov when he offered to fix her car.

Oh fixed Tip's car and then some. He made it fly and powered it with the slushy machine! Tip, Oh, and Pig zoomed through the sky in the newly named Slushious and headed to Paris, where they hoped to learn Tip's mom's location.

At the Great Antenna, which was the Boov name for the Eiffel Tower, Captain Smek got some bad news. The Big Brain Boov still hadn't guessed Oh's e-mail password. And they were running out of time!

"This is number-one disaster!" Captain Smek exclaimed. "His message must not reach the Gorg!"

"I found Oh," Kyle admitted. Kyle had tried to capture Oh, and the fight ended in an explosion. "But I erased him."

Kyle didn't know that Oh actually had escaped with Tip's help! When they reached Paris, Tip and Oh snuck into the Great Antenna to use the giant computer. They wanted to find Tip's mom, but first they needed to stop Oh's e-mail from reaching the Gorg. Time was running out!

Oh entered his password.

"It is, 'MyNameisOhandCaptainSmekisgreatandanyonewhodoesnotthinkthatisapoomp,'" Oh said, then added, "One."

With that, he stopped his e-mail from being sent, moments before the Gorg would have received it!

Next, Oh used the computer to locate Tip's mom. She had been sent to Happy Humanstown, which was in Australia. "What are we waiting for?" Tip said excitedly. "Let's go get her!"

But before Tip and Oh could get back to Slushious, they ran into Captain Smek. And he was not in a forgiving mood. "You has made your mistake. And many mistakes before that. Erase him!" Captain Smek commanded.

"Let us go!" yelled Tip. "Or I will mess with this gravity thingee!"

"She's bluffing," Captain Smek said. "She could not possibly reach—"

Tip stretched as high as she could and grabbed the Gravity Ball!

The Great Antenna began to shake. Then it swung back and forth like an enormous pendulum—slowly at first, then faster and faster, until it started to demolish the city of Paris!

Tip and Oh took advantage of the chaos to escape back to Slushious. As they flew toward Australia, Tip could tell that Oh had something on his mind.

"I am thinking the Boov should never have come to Smekland. To . . . Earth," Oh told her. "So I am saying the sorry to you."

During the long journey Tip and Oh fell asleep. When they awoke, a horrible surprise was waiting for them: Boov Bubble-ships had filled the sky! Tip and Oh screamed in terror!

Then Tip frowned. "Wait. They're not attacking us," she said.

"They are running away," replied Oh. "There can only be one reason."

"Gorg!" Tip exclaimed as a fleet of Gorg ships zipped after the Boov Bubble-ships. Then a Boov ship blew up a Gorg ship! Pieces of the Gorg ship slammed into Slushious, sending it plummeting toward the ground.

After Slushious crashed and stopped working, Tip was worried she would never find her mom. Oh began to sing the Boov death song, but Tip refused to give up. "Look!" she said, pointing at a downed Gorg ship. "Maybe you could use parts from it to fix our car!"

"This has low probability of success," Oh grumbled as Tip dragged him over to the Gorg ship.

To Tip and Oh's relief, the Gorg ship was an empty drone. It didn't have a pilot, so it was safe to look inside!

Oh searched for anything that could fix Slushious. "It is Gorg Super-chip!" he yelled suddenly. "The Slushious will fly again!"

Tip was excited too. "I knew this would all work out!"

The Gorg Super-chip gave Slushious more than enough power to get them to Australia.

When Tip and Oh finally reached Happy Humanstown, Captain Smek and the other Boov were boarding the Boov Mothership, hoping to flee the planet. Oh begged Tip to leave with him, to escape the Gorg, but she refused.

"You will never find her!" Oh said, pleading. "We must run away now!"

"You're just running away because you're a Boov," Tip replied. "I'm not leaving my family."

So Tip went looking for her mom, and Oh boarded the ship—leaving Tip behind.

Wham! Slam! Blam! Blasts from the Gorg fighters rocked the Boov Mothership, which was very low on power, making it impossible to fly away. Then Oh had a great idea. He shoved the Gorg Super-chip into the control panel. Suddenly the Boov Mothership zoomed into the atmosphere!

The other Boov were so impressed by Oh's bravery that they made him their new captain—and even gave him the Shusher!

Back on Earth, Tip couldn't find her mom anywhere. Then Oh returned to help. He used his new tracking device to locate Tip's mom!

"I was so scared I'd never see you again," Tip's mom said, giving Tip a huge hug.

"I never would have stopped looking until I found you, Mom," replied Tip.

"We must demonstrated our affections later," Oh told them, pointing at the sky.

The Gorg Mothership had arrived! And Oh had a funny feeling he knew what it wanted. Seeing Tip hug her mom gave Oh an idea.

"They are still looking, too," he said, holding the Shusher high, "for this!"

When the Gorg finally noticed Oh, the ship ground to a halt, because the Shusher was no ordinary rock. It actually contained millions of Gorg eggs—the next generation of Gorg. That's why the Gorg had been following the Boov around the universe!

The Gorg left as soon as Oh handed over the precious rock. Tip and her mom rushed up to Oh for hugs and high fives . . . and so did everyone else from Happy Humanstown.

Soon after, when Oh finally had his housewarming party, aliens from all over the galaxy came to celebrate. There was no doubt about it: Oh really was a Super Boov!